THE BALLARD DOWN MURDER

Rachel McLean writes thrillers that make your pulse race and your brain tick. Originally a self-publishing sensation, she has sold millions of copies digitally, with massive success in the UK, and a growing reach internationally too. She is the author of the Dorset Crime novels and the spin-off McBride & Tanner series and Cumbria Crime series. In 2021, she won the Kindle Storyteller Award with *The Corfe Castle Murders* and her last five books have all hit No1 in the Bookstat ebook chart on launch.

ALSO BY RACHEL MCLEAN

Dorset Crime series

The Corfe Castle Murders
The Clifftop Murders
The Island Murders
The Monument Murders
The Millionaire Murders
The Fossil Beach Murders
The Blue Pool Murders
The Lighthouse Murders
The Ghost Village Murders
The Poole Harbour Murders
The Chesil Beach Murders
...and more to come

RACHEL MCLEAN

DORSET CRIME SERIES PREQUEL NOVELLA

THE BALLARD DOWN MURDER

ACKROYD PUBLISHING

Copyright © 2022, 2025 by Rachel McLean

All rights reserved.

No part of this book may be reproduced in any form or by any electronic or mechanical means, including information storage and retrieval systems, without written permission from the author, except for the use of brief quotations in a book review.

This is a work of fiction. Names, characters, businesses, places, events and incidents are either the products of the author's imagination or used in a fictitious manner. Any resemblance to actual persons, living or dead, or actual events is purely coincidental.

Ackroyd Publishing

ackroydpublishing.com

Printed and bound in the UK by CPI Group (Uk) Ltd, Croydon CR0 4YY

CHAPTER ONE

Detective Sergeant Dennis Frampton flapped his newspaper open. His wife had laid the kitchen table, the usual Tuesday morning spread: toast and jam, a pot of tea. Tomorrow there would be a boiled egg, Pam's way of marking the middle of the week. And on Saturday, a fry-up.

You had to go a long way to beat Pam's fry-ups as far as Dennis was concerned, and even further since she'd switched to using an air fryer. The olive oil had taken longer to acclimatise to, but he was just about there.

She sat down opposite him and picked up the pot of tea. "Got anything interesting on today, Den?"

He shook his head. "The alleged robbery in Swanage."

"Alleged?"

"I'd lay odds it's an insurance scam. The shop's been trading poorly for months, there were rumours it was about to close."

"Well, we all need to find a way through adversity."

"Not by breaking the law, we don't." He lifted his newspaper higher.

There'd been no witnesses to this robbery, and the CCTV had conveniently been down. He had to follow it up, just in case.

But armed robbers? In Swanage?

It was no more likely than a flock of rowdy seagulls pecking their way into the till and making off with the takings.

"Well, I hope it turns out for the best," she said.

He grunted and placed the last slice of toast in his mouth. He took his handkerchief from his pocket – clean and freshly ironed that morning – and dabbed at his mouth.

"You were up late last night," she reminded him.

"Watching Morse." Dennis liked to watch reruns of *Inspector Morse* on the UK Gold channel. It was his secret vice. Well, almost secret.

He yawned.

"Sorry, love. It's rude of me, I know."

She smiled. "It's fine. Maybe an earlier night tonight?"

He shrugged.

She sipped at her tea. "Well, I'm meeting up with Mary, going shopping in Poole."

"Any particular reason?"

"It's her daughter's birthday next week, she wants new clothes."

Dennis nodded. The thought of spending the day buying clothes for somebody else's daughter was almost as bad as spending it chasing after a non-existent robber.

He pushed back his plate, laid his newspaper on the table in front of it and stood up. He replaced his reading glasses with his bifocals, which had been sitting next to his plate.

"Anyway, best be going."

He rounded the table and kissed Pam on the top of her head.

As he left the dining room, his phone buzzed: a text from his former DCI, Tim Mackie.

Dennis put the phone back in his pocket. He'd rather check it when he was out of the house.

No one knew Dennis was still in touch with Mackie. The occasional social contact had been expected, but this went further. Dennis missed Mackie's experience. The two DCs on his team were good, Johnny Chiles in particular, but neither of them had the old DCI's nose for a case.

Dennis grabbed his tweed jacket from the hook in the hall, slid his slippers off, and put on his shoes. Practical, sturdy shoes, the kind of thing you needed working as a detective in Dorset.

Once outside, he took out his phone and read Mackie's message.

Happy to meet up later. This Superintendent Carpenter's idea?

Dennis frowned. Carpenter knew nothing about this.

All my idea, sir.

His phone buzzed.

You don't have to call me sir. Not now I'm retired.

It would take Dennis a lot more than a few months without Mackie in the office to get used to that.

See you later, he tapped out, hesitating before sending without adding the *sir*.

Yawning again, he placed his phone in the hands-free holder he never used while he was on the move, and pulled the car out of the drive.

CHAPTER TWO

Johnny Chiles was already in the office when Dennis arrived. No sign of Mike Legg yet. Dennis shrugged off his jacket and laid it over the back of his chair. He smoothed out a crease and looked at the DC.

"Cup of tea, Johnny?"

"Please, Sarge." Johnny didn't look up from his screen.

Dennis resisted the urge to berate the younger man on his manners before sighing and heading for the kitchen. One cup for Johnny, strong with two sugars; his own paler with no sugar, part of Pam's health kick. He took the two mugs back to the office to find that Mike had arrived. Dennis checked the clock over the door. One minute late.

"Everything alright, Mike?" he asked.

Mike looked up. "Sorry, Sarge. Traffic on the A35 again."

"Surely by now you'd know to compensate for that?"

"Sorry." Mike turned and looked at the clock. "It was only a minute."

"Hmm." A minute, in this job, could be a lifetime.

"I'll leave you to get your own tea," Dennis said as he

CHAPTER TWO

placed Johnny's mug down. He ignored the shared glance between the two DCs.

"Mine's a coffee, anyway," replied Mike. "But yeah, of course I'll get my own."

Dennis placed his tea on the coaster that lived on his desk and slid into his chair. He shuffled to make himself comfortable, then turned on his computer.

A couple of dozen emails had arrived in the night, most of them dull. He scratched his chin as he worked his way through them. Did he want to spend the day trawling through his inbox, or did he prefer a wild goose chase after these so-called robbers?

He leaned back in his chair. Even non-existent robbers would be more like proper police work than a day at a computer screen.

"Johnny," he said, rising from his chair. "Come with me, let's follow up on that robbery."

Johnny put his mug down, spilling tea on the desk. Dennis waited for him to mop it up, but he didn't.

"You sure, Sarge?" he asked. "I thought you reckoned it was an insurance scam?"

"Doesn't hurt to be thorough," Dennis replied. "Please let Mike know we're heading out. He can deal with the inbox while we're gone."

"Yes, Sarge." Johnny left the room.

Dennis waited, looking at his watch. Mike was the newest member of the team. Cutting his teeth on emails, even six months into the job, would do him good.

CHAPTER THREE

It was eleven o'clock when Dennis and Johnny arrived back at the office. The information the shopkeeper had given them contradicted what he'd said in his original statement, but he was still insisting there had been a robbery. The level of detail he provided was suspicious, and it was clearly difficult for the man to keep it all straight in his head.

Dennis had filled out another statement and given the man his crime number. He imagined the insurance company would spend more time investigating it than he was about to do.

As he and Johnny mounted the stairs towards their first-floor office, a door opened and a young woman came out.

"Detective Sergeant Frampton?" she asked.

"Yes?"

"Superintendent Carpenter would like to speak to you."

Dennis clenched his fist. He was due to be meeting Mackie in two hours. He hoped this wouldn't take long.

"You go back to the office," he told Johnny. "Help DC Legg with the inbox."

CHAPTER THREE

Johnny's body sagged. "Really?"

"Really."

"OK, Sarge."

Johnny trudged away.

Dennis followed the young woman to Superintendent Carpenter's office. He knocked and waited.

"Come in," came a voice.

Dennis cleared his throat and stepped inside. He'd only entered this office twice before. Normally, there was a DI or a DCI buffering him from the super, and that was how he liked it. But right now, with Mackie retired and no replacement found as yet, Dennis was reporting directly to Carpenter.

"Sir," he said, standing ramrod straight in front of the man's desk.

"At ease," replied Carpenter. "You don't have to make like you're in the military with me, you know."

"No, Sir." Dennis allowed his shoulders to relax ever so slightly, but it was impossible to banish the tension from his body. "What can I do for you, Sir?"

Carpenter smiled. "I've got good news." He gestured towards one of the chairs next to Dennis. "Grab a seat, this won't take long."

Dennis perched on the edge of the chair. He tugged at his jacket to straighten it, and patted down his hair. The thin strands on top had a tendency to fly away. He'd caught Pam staring at it, possibly wondering how she'd ended up shackled to such an old man.

Pam still looked young. She looked after herself, dyed her hair. Those trips out with friends were sometimes to hairdressers, or even beauty parlours. Dennis shuddered at the idea of a beauty parlour.

"Good news, Sir?" he said, pulling himself back to the present.

Carpenter was sitting on the sofa beside Dennis. Dennis couldn't see the point of sofas in offices; you could fit a lot more people around a table. But Carpenter's office was bigger than the entire ground floor of Dennis's house, so that wasn't an issue here.

"We found you a new DCI," Carpenter said. "DCI Clarke. Temporary secondment, six months down from West Midlands. She was involved in a terror attack last year, PTSD apparently. She's coming down here for a bit of R&R."

Dennis tried to ignore all the gobbledegook and adjust to the idea of an outsider coming to head up the team. A woman, too.

He swallowed.

Still, it wasn't as if she'd have much to do.

The most excitement they normally got down here was the occasional *alleged* armed robbery and sometimes a fight in Bournemouth or Poole on a Saturday night.

She'd get her R&R for a week or two, find she was bored, and head back home.

"Sir," he said.

"You'll look after her when she arrives, yes? Make sure she settles in."

"Of course, Sir. Can I...?" He looked at the file.

"Best not. Confidential information and all that. I'm sure she'll tell you what you need to know."

Dennis would have preferred to be prepared before the woman arrived. He'd never worked for a woman before. But he was used to Pam managing his life, and all the better for it.

CHAPTER THREE

"I'm sure we'll get on fine, Sir," he said. "Can I ask how long she's been a DCI?"

"Eight years," replied the super. "Very well regarded in West Midlands, she's been heading up a division of Force CID for the last three years. So she'll be well equipped for the Major Crime Investigations Team."

"And when will she be starting?"

"June."

Two months away.

"And in the meantime?" Dennis asked.

"Carry on as you are. You're doing a sterling job leading the team."

"Thank you, Sir."

It was wonderful to be given such praise, of course. But Dennis couldn't help but wish the extra responsibility had come with a pay rise. Or even a promotion.

Carpenter wasn't stupid. He knew that promoting a DS to DI, even acting, when he was three years off retirement would wreak havoc with the pension pot.

No. Instead, it was easier to rely on a man's reluctance to risk rocking the boat. On his loyalty and commitment to doing the best possible job.

It was how things worked, in the modern police force.

Dennis clenched his jaw. "Is that all, Sir?"

"Yes." Carpenter waved him away. "Unless you've got anything else to report?"

He thought about the armed robbery case. "No, Sir. Nothing of interest."

CHAPTER FOUR

Dennis knew he should go back into the office. Johnny and Mike would be expecting him, but he didn't want them seeing the look on his face after his conversation with Superintendent Carpenter. Besides, they'd be on their lunch break soon. Safe for them to assume he was held up in his meeting.

He jabbed at the lift button, muttering under his breath as he waited for it to arrive. It was only one floor down to the ground floor, but the lift was more private. He didn't want any old Tom, Dick or Sheila seeing him as he descended to the reception area.

The lift arrived at last, and Dennis travelled down to the ground floor. He kept his head down as he hurried towards the exit and made it to his car without anyone seeing him.

Once there, he threw himself into the car and took a deep breath. He had to regain control of his nerves.

Carpenter had always been a challenging man to work with. DCI Mackie had told him enough for Dennis to be grateful he didn't report to the man directly. And as for this new woman from the West Midlands... Well, he'd deal with that when he came to it. The prospect of being bossed about by a stranger, and a woman to boot, didn't exactly fill him with joyful anticipation. But he'd known from the moment DCI Mackie had announced his retirement that something like this was coming.

He started the ignition and pulled out of his parking space, then hesitated. He slid back in, stopped the car, and picked up his phone. He wanted to speak to Mackie now, before he got home.

The phone rang out. Dennis scraped the fingernails of his free hand along his thigh. He could sense his heart rate increasing. *Roll on retirement*, he thought. Could he apply to leave early?

Mackie wasn't answering. Dennis hung up and sent his old boss a text.

I'll be at Swanage town car park, 1pm. Let me know if you can't be there.

He could use his lunch break. No one had to know he couldn't do his job without bringing his old mentor in.

After staring at the text for a few moments, he pressed send.

He sat back in his seat, craning his neck to look up at the roof of the car. There was a stain. He frowned: how had that got there?

He missed his commanding officer. He didn't like being in charge, he really didn't like being fully responsible for Johnny and Mike.

So why was he so perturbed about this new DCI coming in? He should be relieved.

He shook his head to clear the brain fog and started the ignition. The drive home would calm his agitation. Pam didn't need to see him like this.

CHAPTER FIVE

Gwen watched her husband across the living room. He was reading the newspaper, searching for crime cases. He might have retired a month ago, but Tim was clearly struggling to leave the job behind.

She put out a hand and pushed the newspaper down.

"Leave it, Tim. You don't have to worry about it now."

He peered at her across the top of the paper. "Worry about what?"

"You're looking for crime reports."

He folded the paper and dropped it to the floor. "Just reading the news."

She raised an eyebrow. "Show me what you were reading."

He leaned down to grab the paper and tossed it across the room at her. She flipped through a few pages. Sure enough, there was a report of an alleged robbery in Swanage.

"Is this one you worked on?" she asked.

He shrugged. "Could be related, not sure."

She put a hand across the table and laid it across his.

CHAPTER FIVE

"Dennis Frampton will take care of things," she said. "You don't need to worry."

"Dennis is doing all this on his own," Tim replied. "They need to bring in a DI until my replacement is appointed."

Tim had been frustrated about this. They'd known about his retirement for a year, but still they hadn't filled the vacancy. Local force politics.

She shook her head, smiling inwardly.

"Tim, it's not your problem. Please."

She stroked his hand. "I can't wait to dance with you again."

He looked up. "Hmm?"

"On the cruise. I've been reading the brochure. Did you know their ballroom floor is almost as big as the one they use for *Strictly*? We'll wow them."

He smiled, his eyes sparkling. "Your foxtrot..."

Gwen nodded. When they'd met, they'd been keen ballroom dancers. The trophies on her dressing table reminded her of it. And of how it had all petered out when he'd joined CID. But now, they had time to enjoy rediscovering the feel of gliding across a dancefloor together. She felt a shudder of anticipation run through her.

Tim's phone buzzed. He looked down and his expression fell.

"Who is it?" Gwen asked, pulling her hand back. His phone was in his lap where she couldn't see it.

"Nothing," he said.

Gwen felt her jaw clench. "Is it Dennis?"

He looked up and blinked at her. "He wants to meet for a pint."

"Just a pint?"

"Yes, love. Just a pint. I'm still allowed to keep in touch with my old colleagues, aren't I?"

"Of course you are."

In truth, she was glad he hadn't left his old colleagues behind. Retirement could be a wrench, particularly from a job as all-encompassing as Tim's. She stood and picked up her mug.

"Say hello to him from me," she said, "and pass on my love to Pam."

He nodded, not looking up. She'd lost his attention.

She stopped next to him.

"We should invite them around one evening, have the two of them for dinner. It would be nice, but no shop talk, yes?"

He looked up.

She bent over and gave him a kiss on the lips. As she pulled away, he squeezed her hand.

"No shop talk, I promise."

CHAPTER SIX

Dennis had been sitting in the car park for half an hour.

He needed to get back to his duties before he was missed. *Sir, where are you?* he thought.

He checked his watch, tapping a foot in the foot well.

Tim Mackie was nothing if not reliable. Dennis had known him as a man he could depend on for twenty years. If he promised to be somewhere, then he would be there.

But Mackie was retired now, with a different pace of life. Dennis knew he was enjoying retirement, savouring the time with his wife Gwen. He'd booked them a cruise, the Norwegian fjords. Dennis wondered what Pam would make of a trip to the fjords.

He blew out a sigh and checked his rear-view mirror. He'd take a stroll around the car park. Mackie might be sitting in his own car, waiting for Dennis.

He heaved himself out of the car and hunched his shoulders against the rain. He squinted to look across the car park. It was half full, not as busy as it would be in high season, but not deserted like it had been in the winter. He paced along the tarmac, checking the cars. Mackie drove a Mondeo; he'd bought it the day he'd retired, hire purchase, and reckoned it would be his last car. Dennis didn't like that idea.

There was no sign of the car. Dennis got his phone out and dialled Mackie. No answer.

He fired off a text.

Sorry, I couldn't wait any longer. Let me know when you'd like to meet.

He plunged his phone into his pocket and returned to his car. He shivered, his hair was wet. He angled the rear-view mirror towards him and pushed it back into place, trying to cover up his bald spot. He glanced around the car park one more time then started the car.

Mackie was busy, he was enjoying his retirement. Dennis needed to stop expecting more of the man.

CHAPTER SEVEN

Dorset Police HQ was an ugly, modern building that looked more like a motorway service station than a police station. It sat alone on the edge of a business park outside Wool. Anybody approaching it was picked up by CCTV.

As Dennis drew closer, he knew that Simon and Harry in the guard cabin would be watching him. They had little to do, sitting there in the middle of nowhere, waiting for cars to arrive, checking people in.

Dennis pulled up and showed them his ID.

"Morning, Sergeant Frampton," Harry said.

"Morning," Dennis replied.

"Grotty day, isn't it?"

"Horrible."

The two men in the hut laughed, although it wasn't funny. They didn't have much to amuse them.

Dennis parked in his usual spot, halfway across the car park. It was easier to find a space here, and besides, the exercise was good for him. Pam had a theory that he should walk a mile for every hour he spent sitting at a desk.

His phone rang; it was Johnny.

"Everything OK, Johnny?"

"Yes, boss. I'm in Blandford Forum at a burglary. Laptop stolen, iPad, the usual."

"Anything I can help with?" Dennis asked.

"The man's getting a bit funny with me, thinks we should be putting more resources onto it."

Dennis frowned.

This was the Major Crime Investigations Team, they shouldn't be dealing with burglaries. But things had been quiet lately, and CID had made use of the extra resource.

He sighed. There was a mountain of paperwork on his desk, and that alleged robbery in Swanage to deal with.

"OK," he said to Johnny. "Text me the address. I'll be there as soon as I can. But we'll have to make it quick."

"Thanks, Sarge."

Twenty minutes later he was in Blandford Forum. It was a market town, populated by attractive Victorian houses mixed in with more modern streets. It would be pretty, if it wasn't being lashed with rain. A squad car was parked outside the house. Dennis got out of his car to see two uniformed PCs outside the front door.

"Morning," he said to them. "Haven't you got anything better to do than stand there?"

"Sorry, Sarge," replied the woman. She glanced at her male colleague. "I'll do door-to-door."

"You do that," said Dennis. "What's your name, anyway?"

"PC Abbott," she replied.

"And I'm PC Mullins," added the man.

Dennis looked at him. "I didn't ask you."

"Sorry, Sarge."

CHAPTER SEVEN

Dennis softened.

He was annoyed because Mackie hadn't turned up, and he wasn't enjoying this weather. It wasn't necessary to take it out on Uniform.

"No. I'm sorry, Constable," he said. "You help your colleague with the door-to-door, let me know if you find anything pertinent. Yes?"

"Pertinent, Sarge?"

"Relevant. Anything that helps identify the burglar."

"Of course. Yes, Sarge." The PC hurried away after his colleague.

The front door to the house was already open. Homeowners who had recently been burgled seemed to ignore security immediately afterwards. It was as if they felt themselves invincible because the police were aware of them. He'd worked one case as a PC where an opportunistic passer-by had slipped into a house while he and his colleague were taking a witness statement and pinched a handbag from the hallway.

He cleared his throat and announced his presence, closing the door behind him.

Johnny's reply came through from the first door. Dennis went through it to find Johnny standing opposite a red-faced man with thinning blond hair. A plump brunette sat on the sofa. She looked embarrassed, eyes down, fingers kneading her thighs.

"Good afternoon, Sir," Dennis said to the man. "I'm Detective Sergeant Frampton. I've just put two uniformed officers on door-to-door inquiries, so hopefully we'll be able to find out more about your break-in. Have you provided a statement to my colleague?"

"We're just in the middle of it, Sarge," Johnny said.

The man opened his mouth to speak, and then closed it again. He looked Dennis up and down.

"So I've got a DS on the case now, have I?"

"Yes, Sir," Dennis replied. "DC Chiles thought it might be helpful for me to get involved as well."

The man grunted. "Good. It's an aggravated burglary, you know."

"In what way was it aggravated?" Dennis asked.

"You go and look at the damage to the window in the back room."

Dennis tried not to roll his eyes.

Men like this liked to watch crime programmes, pick up the lingo. He had no more idea what an aggravated burglary was than he did the difference between a common assault and ABH. Doing damage to a window didn't make an offence aggravated.

Dennis sighed and walked through to the back room. This was going to be a long afternoon.

CHAPTER EIGHT

Dennis slammed the front door shut behind him. It tended to stick in wet weather, he needed to see to that.

He shrugged off his coat and hung it up, then stooped to remove his shoes. Pam kept a tray for muddy boots in the hallway, which meant less time spent sweeping the floors downstairs. Very sensible, in Dennis's opinion.

He walked through to the kitchen where he could smell onions frying.

"Hi, love," he said. "What's for dinner?"

She turned to him. "Bolognese, that OK?"

"Sounds lovely."

He hadn't heard from Mackie all afternoon. He was aware of the phone in his pocket, his itch to keep checking it. He'd sent two more texts and left a voicemail message; he knew he was pestering his old boss. Mackie wasn't on the force any more, he owed Dennis nothing. But the two of them had agreed to meet, and Dennis had never known the man to be unreliable.

"Everything OK?" Pam asked, frowning at him.

He shook his head. "It's nothing. Nothing to worry about."

She turned the hob down and stopped stirring the onions. "You don't look like it's nothing."

"It's fine," he said, meeting her gaze. "Just work stuff."

She rolled her eyes. "One of these days your job will get less stressful."

"That'll be the day I retire."

"Talking of which," she said, "I got a phone call from Gwen Mackie this afternoon. She's invited us for dinner tomorrow night."

He felt a lump form in his throat. "Gwen Mackie?"

"Yes. You look like you've seen a ghost. Den, what's wrong?"

"Did she say where her husband was?"

Pam frowned. "No, why? Are you worried about him?"

"I'm not sure," said Dennis. "He was supposed to meet me at lunchtime today, but he didn't turn up. It's not like him."

She shrugged and turned the hob back on. "He's retired, you have to make allowances. You're not involving him in cases, are you?"

"No."

With her back towards him, Pam hadn't noticed Dennis look away. "Why don't you go and put the fire on while I finish this?"

He nodded and left the kitchen. As he entered the living room, his phone rang. It was a call from the office. This could only be bad news.

"DS Frampton," he said.

"Sarge, this is PC Abbott. Sorry to interrupt your

evening. Superintendent Carpenter has asked me to call you."

He glanced at the clock on the mantelpiece. Half past six.

"What's the situation?" he asked, feeling a chill run down the back of his neck.

"I'm at the top of the cliffs, north of Swanage, towards Ballard Down. The CSIs are on their way and the Coast Guard have been called out."

Dennis drew in a shaky breath.

"Why?" he asked. "Tell me what's happened, PC Abbott."

"A body has been found," she said. "At the base of the cliffs."

CHAPTER NINE

Dennis stopped to check in with the uniformed PC on duty at the farm gate.

"DS Frampton, where do I need to go?"

The PC turned away and pointed. "You can park in the farmyard. There's a gate that takes you through to the coastal path. Farmer says to make sure you lock it."

Dennis grunted and closed his window. He knew how farmers could react if the police didn't close gates behind them. They were lucky the farmer had allowed them access via his land; it would be at least a mile further if they'd been forced to park on the main road.

He followed a track and pulled up behind two squad cars and the CSI van. He wondered how long the CSIs had beaten him by.

Opening the car door, he was hit by the rain hammering into his skin. He slammed the door and hurried to the boot for his coat. It was his thickest waterproof, a Christmas present from Pam.

He threw it on, huddling against the wind. Rain blew

CHAPTER NINE

across the farmyard, ripples skidding over puddles. A security light on the back of a barn illuminated the space. He peered around, a hand shielding his eyes, and spotted a gate with crime scene tape attached to it. The tape was being whipped by the wind; it wouldn't last long.

He grappled with the bolt to open the gate and closed it behind him. He wondered where the farmer was. It was almost fully dark now, the field ahead of him disappearing into the gloom.

He zipped his coat up higher and brought his torch out of a pocket. Thank goodness he was wearing sensible shoes.

He made his way forwards, following a muddy path. He walked slowly, aware that the cliffs were somewhere in front of him.

After perhaps two minutes of walking, he caught a glimpse of lights moving up ahead. He carried on towards them until he reached the coastal path.

Two uniformed constables were erecting a cordon, and a white-suited tech was leaning over the bushes separating the paths from the sea below.

Dennis realised he should have called Johnny.

Never mind. He'd speak to the CSIs first.

One of the Uniforms turned towards him. It was the same young woman he'd dealt with earlier that day.

"Sarge," she said, "there's a body been found at the bottom of the cliffs." She pointed towards the CSI. "We don't know if it was washed up, or if the person fell."

"Or worse," said Dennis. He approached the bushes and peered over. He couldn't see anything; it was too dark.

"What have we got?" he asked the tech.

The CSI straightened up. "I'm looking for any sign of disturbance in these bushes."

"Who found the body?" He caught himself. "Is it a body, or are we looking at a rescue operation?"

"Coastguard are on their way. He was spotted by a couple of walkers further along. Apparently they watched while they waited for us to arrive. No sign of movement."

"That doesn't mean anything."

"No."

The female PC was behind him. "Sarge."

Dennis turned. "What's your name again?"

She smiled. "PC Abbott, Sarge."

"Any sign of a struggle up here?"

PS Abbott exchanged glances with the CSI. "Not that we've found."

"But this wind..." added the CSI.

"Gav's right," the PC added. "I don't think we'll get much until the morning."

"I'll judge that, thank you very much," Dennis told her. She pursed her lips.

He turned towards the CSI. The man was tall, and Dennis had to crane his neck.

"What are you looking for?" Dennis asked.

"Signs of disturbance on the grass," he said. "Damage to the shrubs up here. I know the weather isn't any help, but that's all the more reason to get what we can as soon as we can."

"And?"

"No sign of damage to the shrubs yet."

"Footprints?"

"It's too dark."

"You've got lights, haven't you?"

The CSI sniffed. "We've had two PCs, you and me up here. Could have been others, before we got here."

CHAPTER NINE

"Surely that's the point."

The CSI shook his head. "We've cordoned off the area above the spot where the body is, there are clear boot prints up there. Nothing distinct along here, or in the other direction."

"So you've got prints on the edge but nothing leading to them?"

"I didn't say that. There's too much leading to them, the ground's all churned up. Too much mud, too—"

"I'd have thought mud would help."

"Depends on the kind of mud. Sorry."

Dennis sighed. He caught a light out to sea, heading their way. "I hope that's the coastguard."

"They're on their way. Gail's with them."

Gail Hansford was the crime scene manager. Dennis found her irritating, but he couldn't deny she was good at her job.

"Sorry," he said. "What's your name again?"

"Gavin Larcomb. I worked on the—"

"Don't worry. I'm not very good with names."

The CSI raised his eyebrows.

"I've got something!"

Dennis and the CSI looked up. The male PC was at the other end of the cordon, gesturing towards them.

Gavin hurried towards him. Dennis followed, less hasty. He didn't want to risk falling.

"What is it, Constable?" he asked.

"More footprints," the PC said. He pointed with his torch. Sure enough, there were clear prints in the mud, leading towards the shrubs.

"They're not ours?" Dennis asked.

"We'll make sure we've got footwear details for everyone

here, for elimination purposes," the CSI said. "Well spotted, Constable."

The PC smiled.

"What's your name, lad?" Dennis asked.

The constable straightened. "PC Mullins, Sarge."

"Good. You stay here, make sure no one goes near those prints."

"Of course."

The light of the coastguard boat was approaching. Dennis still couldn't hear the engine over the wind.

"How long will it take them?" he asked.

"No idea," the CSI replied. "Gail says the current's against them."

The clouds were clearing out to sea. The boat was visible now, approaching the cliffs beneath them. Beyond it, a new bank of cloud was building past Swanage, over Peveril Point.

Dennis still hadn't called Johnny. They needed two of them on this. He was still hoping that the person at the base of the cliffs was alive. But alive or dead, there would have to be an investigation.

"Very well," he said. "I need to make a call." He'd go back to his car, there was no way he could make himself heard up here. "Let me know if you find anything."

"Will do," the CSI replied. He went back to his work.

CHAPTER TEN

Gwen Mackie checked the clock for the hundredth time. Twelve minutes had passed since the last time she'd looked.

She sighed and pushed herself up from the sofa, making for the kitchen. She flicked the kettle on: anything to distract herself.

Tim hadn't said what time he would be home, but he'd left the house late morning. Meeting Dennis for a pint during the DS's lunch hour, he'd said.

Even if he'd gone for a walk afterwards, he'd be long since home by now.

She checked her watch. Eight o'clock.

Tim, where are you?

She went to the hall table where she kept her phone and unplugged it. She dialled his number.

Voicemail.

She'd already left him three messages. No point in leaving another.

Maybe she should call Dennis?

She opened up the contacts, then realised she didn't have

Dennis Frampton's number. Tim had it stored in his own phone.

She put the phone down and plugged it in again, trying to ignore the fact that her hands were shaking.

Maybe Tim had left his phone at home?

She went into the dining room, to Tim's desk. He hardly used it, now he'd retired.

The desk was clear, tidy. Everything in its place. No phone.

She opened the drawers, realising that her movements were becoming frantic.

Calm down. Panicking wouldn't bring him home.

Tim was a grown man. If he wanted to go out with an old friend for a walk or a drink afterwards, then that was his business. It wouldn't be the first time.

But why hadn't he called her?

The drawers were almost as neat as the top of the desk. No sign of a phone.

She returned to the hall and grabbed her own phone. She dialled Tim's number again, straining to listen.

If he'd left it here, it would ring out. Wouldn't it?

No. She'd already left him three messages. After the first one, if the phone wasn't in use, it would go straight to voicemail without ringing out.

Even if the phone was here, she wasn't going to find it.

Her chest clenched.

She placed her phone back on the table and balled her fist. She was chewing her bottom lip.

She hurried up to the bedroom. Maybe he'd left it on his bedside table?

That too was tidy. A book, his reading glasses.

She sat down on the bed, her limbs heavy.

CHAPTER TEN

This would be nothing. He'd get home at nine o'clock just like he'd always done when he'd gone for a drink after work.

He'd just forgotten to call her. Maybe his phone was out of juice.

But he hadn't gone for a drink after work, had he?

She swallowed. Her throat was tight.

Should she call 999?

She didn't want to be a nuisance. She'd heard enough stories of those over the years.

No. She wasn't a nuisance.

Her husband wasn't home, he wasn't answering his phone, and it was blowing a gale.

She descended the stairs, focusing on keeping her breathing steady. At the bottom, she picked up her phone.

CHAPTER ELEVEN

The two uniformed constables had stationed themselves at either end of their cordon. There were no signs of any passers-by, nobody stupid enough to come up here on such an evil night. The farmer was tucked up safe in his farmhouse. Sensible man.

Johnny was on his way, but he lived almost an hour away. Dennis wondered whether calling him out had been the right thing to do. It was gone 8:00 pm, and night had long since fallen. Gavin Larcomb, the CSI, was still examining the scene. Dennis couldn't believe he'd find anything. Not now.

The coastguard's boat was somewhere below them, out of sight beneath the cliffs. Dennis stamped his feet and clapped his hands together, wishing he'd brought gloves. The rain hadn't let up and his coat was being sorely tested.

The CSI was working his way methodically across the grass. Two more uniformed constables had turned up, and another CSI. They were all assisting in the search.

Dennis watched from a distance, jiggling his shoulders to try and keep warm.

CHAPTER ELEVEN

The first CSI, Gavin, stood up. He held a phone to his ear and was shouting into it against the wind.

Dennis approached him.

"Have you found something?"

Gavin turned to Dennis. He held out his phone.

"You need to take this."

Dennis grabbed the phone from him. "DS Frampton."

"Dennis, it's Gail. I'm with the coastguard."

Dennis frowned. He knew the CSIs weren't expected to address him by his rank, but he found their easy familiarity galling.

"Where?" he asked.

"On the boat. Below you."

Dennis frowned. "How did you get there so quickly?"

"Don't worry about that now. I live right by their station in Swanage, I wanted to see what was happening."

"We can't see you."

"No. And you shouldn't, it's not safe on the cliff edge."

"What have you found?"

"I'm really sorry, Dennis."

He felt his shoulders slump. "A body?"

"We've managed to get on shore," she said. "The tide's gone out a little."

Dennis approached the cliff edge.

"Sarge!" called PC Abbott. "You shouldn't—"

Dennis turned to her. "I'm fine." But she was right. He pulled back.

"Gail," he said. "The victim. Are they alive?"

"No."

"Did they fall, or drown? Can you tell?"

"We'll need the pathologist to attend for that," she replied.

"Sorry?" He plugged his free ear with a finger.

"I said we'll need the pathologist."

"Yes." There was no way Henry Whittaker was going out on the coastguard's boat. "You'll have to move him onto the beach. Is it a him?"

"Yes. And moving him is easier said than done."

"I can't see anything." It wasn't safe to move any closer to the edge. "Have you got an ID?"

"Not formally," Gail replied. "He doesn't have any identifying documents on him."

"But?" Dennis said, sensing that there was something she wasn't telling him.

"I recognise him," Gail said.

Dennis felt his chest clench.

His mind went over the text messages he'd been sending all day.

Could it be...?

No. It was a ridiculous thought.

"Who is it?" he asked the CSM, his throat tight.

"I'm sorry, Dennis."

"Just tell me. Who is it?"

"It's your old DCI," she said. "DCI Mackie."

CHAPTER TWELVE

Dennis closed his eyes and pulled in a breath as he waited for the front door of DCI Mackie's house to be opened.

He'd never been inside the house. He'd waited outside a few times, stopping here occasionally to give the DCI a lift when they were travelling on a case. And although he'd met DCI Mackie's wife Gwen, it had only been briefly, and standing in the driveway.

He wished he'd taken the time to get to know the woman better. That might make what he was about to do a little easier.

He clenched his hands by his sides, opening and closing them, squeezing the flesh of his palms. His throat was tight, his neck stiff. He'd been tense, sitting in an uncomfortable position in the car on the way here, only realising when he pulled up outside. He was still struggling to believe what Gail had told him.

The door opened and Gwen stood in front of him. She was pale, her eyes sunken.

Dennis felt his chest fall. So she already knew.

"DS Frampton," she said. "Come in."

He gave her a tight smile and wiped his feet on the doormat as he passed her. There hadn't been a squad car outside. Had Uniform been and gone? Why hadn't anybody told him?

He walked into the living room to find a familiar face looking at him, its owner occupying what looked like the most comfortable chair in the room.

Dennis straightened, almost standing to attention. The man shook his head.

"It's alright, DS Frampton. You don't need to be formal with me tonight."

Dennis nodded but didn't relax.

"Sir," he said. "I didn't know you were..."

Superintendent Carpenter stood up. "I felt it was important that Mrs Mackie knew as soon as possible. But thank you for coming, DS Frampton. It was the right thing to do."

Gwen Mackie was in the doorway. "Can I get you another cup of tea, Superintendent? DS Frampton?"

Carpenter took a step forward. "DS Frampton will do that for us, won't you, Dennis?"

Dennis felt his cheek twitch. "Of course." He followed Gwen's arm, pointing towards the kitchen. "Thank you," she muttered. He grunted at her, all the words he'd prepared gone from his head.

In the kitchen, he stared around the room. It was neat and tidy, just as he'd imagined. The kettle was in one corner but there was no sign of a tea caddy or cups. He started opening and closing doors.

"Here, Dennis," came a voice, "I can do that."

He turned to see Gwen Mackie standing in the doorway

CHAPTER TWELVE

again. "You don't mind me calling you Dennis, do you? It's just that Tim..." She looked away.

He took a step towards her. "Mrs Mackie. I'm so sorry for your loss."

She grabbed his hands, squeezing them between her own. He resisted the urge to pull away.

"You and Tim were close," she said.

He blinked back at her. *Hold it together, man.*

"DCI Mackie was a good man. An excellent officer. Without him, I wouldn't be... well, I probably never would have joined CID."

She smiled, her eyes sad.

"He talked about you a lot." She dropped his hands and walked to the kettle. Dennis had filled it with water but not switched it on. She flicked it on and took three mugs out of a cupboard, her expression blank.

"Weren't you supposed to be meeting him today?"

Dennis pulled in a breath. He glanced towards the doorway.

"Something like that."

She turned to him. "That's nice. I worried that he'd be a bit lost when he retired, but he still had you."

Had, Dennis noted. They were already talking in the past tense. How was she holding it together so well? Shock, probably.

"I'll make that cup of tea," he said. "You go and sit down. The family liaison officer will be here soon, they'll look after you."

She looked down at the linoleum floor then up and towards the door. Dennis hadn't heard the front door; Carpenter was still in the living room.

"Thank you, Dennis," she said. "I'm glad you're here."

CHAPTER THIRTEEN

Gail Hansford was cold.

She'd wrapped up in her warmest coat and had leggings under her trousers. But even so, out there at sea in this weather, it had been bloody freezing. She watched the coastguard guys as they chugged back in towards Swanage. The wind was dying down now, the rain slowing to drizzle. The coastguards were bulked up, prepared. Proper waterproof gear.

She shivered.

"Do you need to take any more kit out there?" one of them asked her. She knew the two men's names, had worked with them both before. But the shock of turning over the victim's face to see Tim Mackie staring back at her...

Her mind was blank.

Did she need more kit?

Yes. She should get one of her team over here, with the van. She'd run to the coastguard station from home, carrying nothing more than the clothes she was standing in. The

CHAPTER THIRTEEN

coastguard hadn't been prepared to wait, what with the chance that the victim might be alive.

"Let me make a call," she said. "My team are parked up above Ulwell. It won't take long for them to bring what I need."

If they were going to leave Mackie out there until the pathologist arrived, she'd have to protect the body. Erecting a tent would be impossible on those rocks, but she had a kind of bivouac she could use.

"That gives us time to refuel and check the boat over. But we can't hang around."

Gail nodded and wrapped her arms around herself. "I know."

Ten minutes later, the boat was safely at the top of its ramp and she was stomping her feet, standing next to the boathouse. She pulled out her phone and called Brett with instructions.

She turned at the sight of headlamps from the corner of her eye. A car was snaking its way through the boatyard, not an easy challenge in the dark. It stopped next to her and Dr Henry Whittaker got out.

Gail checked her watch. 10:30 at night: this wasn't like him.

"Evening, Doctor."

"I hear you've got a body under the cliffs at Ballard Down."

"Have you been told who it is yet?"

He nodded. "I came as soon as I could."

He certainly had done. Whittaker would have had to drive to Sandbanks and get the ferry across the mouth of Poole Harbour. He must have had the call right after she'd spoken to Dennis.

"Superintendent Carpenter was eager for me to attend as soon as possible."

Gail sniffed. Whittaker didn't do this for most victims. But then, when a retired detective died, it was different for all of them.

"We'll be heading out soon," she told him. "I just need to wait for some kit and the coastguard have to check their boat over. You're coming?"

He looked out to sea. The wind was in his face, making him squint.

"I should have brought a better coat."

"The coastguard might have something they can lend you," she told him.

"I'd appreciate that, if you don't mind."

"I'm sure if you ask them..."

He looked at her. "Oh. Very well." He walked past her and approached the boathouse.

Gail watched him. Had he been expecting her to ask them for a coat for him, as if she were his mum?

Still. At least he was here.

Her phone rang: Dorset Police's Marine Section. They'd be sending out two boats, with divers to check there were no other victims in the water.

"And look for evidential items for me too, please," she said.

"Like what?"

"A weapon. Anything out of place in the area around the victim."

DCI Mackie had shown no signs of having been attacked with a weapon, but it had been dark and they hadn't removed his clothes. And she wasn't a pathologist, after all. She had no idea what might have killed him.

CHAPTER THIRTEEN

"Very well," came the reply.

She hung up to see Whittaker emerge from the boathouse in a coat that was comically large on him. He shuffled along, tugging at it.

"That's better," she said. "Practical."

He grunted. "No idea how I'll work in this get-up. Better than freezing my fingers off, I suppose."

She nodded. He adjusted the gloves he'd been lent. He'd have to remove those to work; his fingers were still at risk of freezing.

The CSI van pulled up behind Whittaker's car. Gail opened the back and pulled out a large bag.

"You want me to come with you?" Brett asked as he helped her haul the bag towards the boat.

"No thanks, mate. Not enough space for me and Whittaker on those rocks, let alone you too."

"The tide's turning in twenty minutes."

"Then we'd better get a move on."

She turned to see the larger of the two coastguard guys holding out a hand to take the bag. She handed it to him.

"Ready?" he asked.

"Ready."

"Good. We need to hurry."

CHAPTER FOURTEEN

Gwen Mackie's hands were chilly. She clasped them between her knees as she sat motionless on the sofa.

Dennis Frampton and Superintendent Carpenter had told her not to get up when they'd left, and she hadn't had the heart to argue. The family liaison officer, a female PC who'd introduced herself as Claire, was rustling around in the kitchen, making herself busy.

Gwen knew how family liaison officers worked; Tim had talked to her about it often enough. Their official job was to provide support and make endless cups of tea. But she knew that really this Claire – PC Kane – was a spy, here to relay Gwen's conversations with family or friends to the investigating team. To find out if Gwen had anything to do with Tim's death.

She gritted her teeth.

The idea that Gwen would have wanted her husband dead was horrific.

The idea that he wasn't going to be walking back in through that door later on was worse.

CHAPTER FOURTEEN

The base of her throat was heavy, making her feel like she might choke.

Tim, she thought, *what happened to you?*

How did a man who'd managed to get through an entire career in the police reach retirement and then find himself dead at the foot of some cliffs?

And as if there wasn't enough to deal with, she could tell by the look in Carpenter's eyes that he thought Tim had killed himself.

Gwen knew better than that.

Tim had been anticipating retirement, he'd been eager to leave his job. He'd paid for that cruise around the Norwegian Fjords that they were going to take in September. They were going to take up dancing again.

They had everything ahead of them. Long, happy years together.

They weren't like most couples of their age, where retirement meant avoiding each other, finding separate rooms in the house to spend time in. Taking up hobbies so they wouldn't be under each other's feet.

For them, retirement was a blessing. It meant time together, time they'd lost while Tim had been on the force.

Gwen closed her eyes. She had no idea how she was going to get through the next few hours.

What time was it anyway?

She'd be expected to go to bed, the family liaison officer would be reporting back. And then...

How was she expected to sleep with the bed empty beside her?

Gwen sat back on the sofa, her eyes closed.

She wanted to cry but the tears wouldn't come. Her face

felt hot and itchy. She wanted to scratch the skin off; anything to distract herself.

She balled her fists, her hands still between her knees.

Tim, she thought, *why did you leave me?*

CHAPTER FIFTEEN

THE TIDE WAS TURNING as they approached the cliffs again; they would have to be quick. Gail turned to Whittaker and shouted to him across the wind.

"How much of an examination will you need to do in situ?"

He shrugged. "Depends on how much I can see. If cause of death is obvious, then it'll be quick. I won't remove any clothing, though."

She nodded. She'd seen plenty of victims in states of undress. Sometimes, they'd lost clothes before being found; other times it had been necessary to remove garments to examine them more thoroughly, even at the crime scene. But this was Tim Mackie. A man she'd worked with. A man she'd assisted on dozens of cases. The thought of grappling with his clothes at the bottom of a cliff in the wind and rain felt disrespectful.

"I know what you're thinking," Whittaker said. "It's not often we know the victim. I'll be careful."

"Good."

The boat moored in the shallows and they climbed into the inflatable again. This time, she was quicker, knowing the drill. Even Whittaker's movements were smooth and practised. The man was surprising her tonight.

The water was higher against the rocks, rising towards where Mackie's body lay. The tarpaulin she'd draped over him had shifted and his legs were visible. She pulled the tarp away, watching Whittaker's face. His jaw hardened.

She hesitated, giving him a moment. She'd needed one too, after turning Mackie's head over to recognise the face. It had been such a shock that she'd almost fallen back into the water.

After a moment, she cleared her throat. "We need to be quick."

"Of course." Whittaker bent over to get a better look, bringing a small torch out of his pocket. "Not easy to see much out here though."

Gail turned to the coastguard. "Can we take him ashore tonight?"

"That's what you want to do?"

Gail exchanged looks with Whittaker. It was normal procedure to leave a body in place until a thorough examination had taken place. Not just of the body, but of the surrounding area too. But this was far from a normal crime scene.

Whittaker nodded, his jaw still hard.

"It is," she said. "The sea could wash him out if we don't."

"OK. You prepare him for removal, we'll set up the winch."

CHAPTER FIFTEEN

Gail swallowed. Whittaker was crouched on the rocks, putting out a hand to steady himself every time the wind blew. She was glad of the coastguard men behind them, ready in case they should be swept into the sea by a gust of wind.

She reached into the bag she'd brought and took out her camera. She moved around the body as best she could, firing off photos. Her hands were stiff on the shutter button and her body felt rigid as she worked, and not just from the cold. Whittaker shifted to one side so she could get an angle, then went back to work. It wasn't ideal, having the pathologist on the edge of the crime scene photos. But then, nothing about this crime scene was ideal.

When she'd finished, she looked at Whittaker. "What do you think?"

He looked up. "I can't determine anything obvious."

"Was he alive or dead when he fell?"

Whittaker turned back towards the body. He shook his head. "Judging by the positioning of the limbs, I think in all probability he was alive. But I wouldn't swear to it. His legs have landed in a way that would be impossible if rigor mortis had set in, but that doesn't mean he wasn't recently dead."

"So the fall might not have killed him?"

"I'm not speculating just yet."

She gazed over the pathologist's shoulder at the body. She wondered if Dennis was at the man's house already, informing his wife. Widow. Poor woman. Did Mackie have a family, she wondered?

Whittaker straightened up, a hand in the small of his back. He winced.

"Are you OK?" she asked.

He smiled grimly. "Probably wasn't the best idea to come out here tonight. I'm not as young as you. But, well..."

"I know."

"Probably a waste of time. There isn't much I can determine here. We'll have to take him back to Poole for a full post-mortem. I'll be able to tell you more then."

CHAPTER SIXTEEN

Dennis was getting into his car as he heard his name being called.

"DS Frampton, a word please."

He turned back to see Superintendent Carpenter closing the front door of the Mackie house. The family liaison officer, PC Kane, was in there already. Her job was to look after Gwen Mackie, to relieve some of the burden, but also to tell them if anything pertinent happened inside that house.

Dennis still couldn't believe that DCI Mackie was dead. Gail hadn't described the condition of his body yet, but in the morning there would be crime scene photos. The board in Mackie's old office would have to be brought into use.

He clenched his toes inside his shoes. How could they possibly use DCI Mackie's office as the base for an investigation into the man's death?

No, he thought, he would bring the board out into the main office. He couldn't do it in there.

But then there would be no privacy. The photos would be on display for anybody to see.

He'd requisition a meeting room. This was a special case after all.

"DS Frampton," Carpenter asked, "are you alright?"

Dennis blinked a few times and looked up at Superintendent Carpenter, standing in front of him.

"Sorry, Sir," he replied, straightening his back. "Miles away."

Carpenter gave him a sympathetic smile.

"I can understand, Sergeant. I gather you and DCI Mackie were close."

Dennis felt sharpness behind his eyes. *Don't let it get to you.* He needed to be professional.

"Who will be the SIO?" he asked.

"I'd like to bring in someone from another team, possibly another force."

"The new DCI, the woman you told me about?"

Carpenter shook his head. "She's still needed in the West Midlands."

Dennis nodded.

"But in the meantime," Carpenter said, "I need you to kick off this investigation. We'll get the pathologist's report as quickly as we can and we'll put this to bed. It's a tragedy that DCI Mackie killed himself, but—"

Dennis jerked his head up. "Killed himself, Sir?"

Carpenter frowned. "Well, yes, man. What else do you think happened?"

Dennis stared at the senior officer.

"But DCI Mackie... He would never do that, Sir. He knew what it was like for the individuals who found a suicide victim. He'd seen it himself. He even talked about it. There's no chance—"

"Well if he didn't kill himself, Sergeant, that means some-

CHAPTER SIXTEEN

body must have pushed him, and do you really think that happened?"

Dennis clenched a fist.

"Nobody would want DCI Mackie dead. But..." He drew in a breath, realising it was more of a gasp. "I'll brief my team in the morning, Sir. I'll kick things off."

Carpenter nodded.

"It'll be a straightforward case, DS Frampton. Suicide. Poor chap couldn't handle retirement. Once we get the pathologist's report, I'm sure the coroner will agree."

CHAPTER SEVENTEEN

The meeting room was small and smelt of damp and sawdust. But it was better than running this investigation in DCI Mackie's office, and it was certainly better than having that board out in the open.

Dennis positioned the board so it was facing away from the door. He didn't want people barging in and seeing the photos. It had already taken him five minutes to pluck up the courage to look at them himself. They'd arrived in an envelope in the night, placed discreetly on his desk.

Gail Hansford knew how sensitive this case was, how Dennis and his team would feel about it. Gail could be annoying at times, but she knew when to tread carefully.

He leaned on the table in the centre of the room and stared at the board, his eyes glazing over. The crime scene photos showed Mackie's body slumped at the bottom of the cliff, his limbs splayed. His head faced upwards but that wasn't how he'd been found; he'd been face-down when Gail had first arrived at the scene. A novice CSI might have moved his head back into its original position, try to recreate the scene as they'd found it. But Gail knew the less you disturbed a body, the better.

There were photos in better light too, taken before Gail had moved Mackie's head. These were lower quality, taken on a mobile phone. They showed Mackie from out to sea, his body crumpled into the rocks.

Dennis pushed out a breath. He felt sick.

Yet more photos showed the clifftop above. The ones from the night before showed the whole scene, no detail. The CSIs had been back at dawn and taken more photos, close-ups of boot prints. They still needed to check which belonged to the officers and CSIs who'd been present, and which were of interest. The farmer would have to provide boot prints too, to rule him out.

One set of prints, which as yet hadn't been matched to any of the elimination prints, led in a straight line to the cliff edge. A single line of footprints, heading straight for the cliffs. Nothing coming back again.

If those were Mackie's, then they'd been the last steps he'd taken. If they belonged to someone else, there would have been a set leading back. And no one had gone that close to the edge. The cordon had made sure of that.

Dennis stared at the prints, his heart heavy.

Sir, why did you do it?

If somebody had pushed him, there would be more than one set of footprints. The only explanation for a pattern like that was suicide.

It made no sense.

Dennis had met Mackie in the pub on a few occasions since his retirement. Mackie had been at ease, revelling in the lack of stress now that he wasn't heading up the Major Crime

Investigations Team. If anything, he'd been smug. Encouraging Dennis to retire early.

His marriage was solid. Better than solid. He and Gwen had been looking forward to spending time together. They'd booked a holiday.

Mackie had been helping Dennis with the robbery case. He'd been happy to do so. He'd been interested, but not in a way that made Dennis think the man was missing his old life.

Dennis gripped the top of the desk.

Did this have something to do with that case? Had Mackie regretted getting involved in old cases when he wasn't supposed to?

Had somebody threatened him?

The door opened and Johnny walked in.

"Morning, Sarge." He glanced at Dennis then looked down at the floor.

"Morning, Johnny," Dennis replied. "You've heard?"

Johnny clenched his jaw. "Terrible news."

Dennis nodded. "It is, Constable, but we've got a job to do." He gestured towards the board. "These aren't easy viewing."

"They've made you SIO?"

"Temporarily. They're bringing in someone from outside. Although I don't think they'll need to." He gestured at the photo of the single line of prints.

Johnny winced. "Shit."

"Johnny."

"Sorry, Sarge. I'll stick a quid in your swear jar."

"I'll let you off. Just this once."

"Sarge. You just be—"

"We have a job to do, Johnny. I suggest we get on with it."

CHAPTER SEVENTEEN

The door opened again and Dennis looked round to see DC Mike Legg enter.

"Mike," he said.

"Sarge. I heard about the DCI."

Dennis turned away from him.

Mike approached the board. "They haven't seriously given us the investigation?"

"Temporarily," Dennis and Johnny replied in unison.

"Good. It's not exactly..." Mike cocked his head, peering at the photo of the prints. "What's that?"

Dennis sighed. "We'll need to check it out, but it looks like the prints of someone who walked to the edge then stepped off."

Mike looked at him, his eyes wide. "Just stepped off?"

Dennis nodded.

"Just like that?" Mike looked at Johnny. "The DCI would never do that."

"That's what I was thinking," said Johnny.

"The evidence would suggest otherwise," Dennis added.

Johnny sat down next to Dennis. "I know the evidence says it, Sarge. But you knew the DCI better than anyone. Would he really have done something like this?"

"Who's keeping an eye on the office, while...?" asked Mike.

"Don't worry," Dennis told him. "I've asked the main switchboard to take all our calls."

"Good," Mike replied.

Johnny put a hand on Dennis's shoulder.

"You alright, Sarge?"

Dennis shrugged off his hand.

"I'll be fine, Johnny," he said, ignoring the catch in his

voice. "Let's just get on with the case." He pointed at the board. "It's *looking* like suicide…"

Mike lowered himself into a chair. The three men sat in silence for a moment, contemplating the photos or paying their respects, Dennis wasn't sure which.

"So we definitely think it's suicide?" Mike asked.

Dennis flinched. "That's what the super reckons."

Johnny turned to him. "But you don't?"

"The forensics point that way," Dennis said. "But DCI Mackie wasn't suicidal. I met the man for a drink last week. He was… happy."

"Sometimes people pretend," Mike replied.

He had a point. DCI Mackie might have been putting up a front.

Dennis swallowed. "Anyway," he said. "We need to get to work. I want more photos from a higher angle. See if the route of those prints lines up with where Mackie was found."

"Shall I…?" asked Johnny.

"Yes. You go to the clifftop. Speak to Gail Hansford. And Mike, I want the post-mortem report chasing up. We need to know what Whittaker thinks."

CHAPTER EIGHTEEN

Gwen hovered in her kitchen, watching the family liaison officer pour water into the kettle. She had nothing to do and it made her feel uneasy.

"Let me do that, please," she said.

The young woman turned to her and smiled.

"It's OK, Mrs Mackie. I'm here to help you."

Yes, but that doesn't help.

Gwen balled her fist and placed it on the kitchen worktop.

"Have you heard any news?" she asked, as the woman flicked on the kettle.

PC Kane turned to her. "Sorry, Mrs Mackie, nothing as yet."

"Nothing from the pathologist?"

A shake of the head.

"He went out there last night," Gwen said. "DS Frampton told me."

The young woman looked into Gwen's eyes, as if trying to judge how much she should say.

"It's alright," Gwen said. "I'm used to this kind of thing. I want to know everything."

The PC bit her bottom lip. "The coastguard took the pathologist and the CSM, that's the crime scene manager, to the scene last night. They would have examined your husband's body. There hasn't been an official report on the cause of death yet, but..."

"I know," said Gwen. "The fall from the cliffs. The question is, how did it happen?"

The PC shook her head. "I'd rather not speculate, Ma'am, if you don't mind?"

"Of course not."

Gwen raked her fingernails against the worktop.

"Where's Superintendent Carpenter? Is he going to come back here, or will it be Dennis?"

"I'm expecting DS Frampton," the PC replied.

"Good."

Gwen had felt uneasy with Carpenter in her home. There was something off about the man, something that kept her from trusting him. He was too posh for Dorset, to start with.

The doorbell rang and PC Kane dried her hands on a tea towel that Gwen didn't remember taking from the cupboard.

"You wait here, Ma'am, I'll get it."

Gwen watched the young woman leave the room, feeling like a stranger in her own house.

She didn't like this. It wasn't as if she had things to do, things that the PC was taking away from her. All the woman had done was clean the kitchen a few times and make two dozen cups of tea.

Voices came from the hallway. Gwen stepped out of the kitchen to see Dennis Frampton standing in the doorway, shrugging off his coat. The PC took it from him and hung it on a hook, glancing at Gwen to check as she did so. Gwen nodded.

"Morning, Dennis," she said, as he wiped his feet on the mat.

"Morning, Mrs Mackie," he replied. "How are you today?"

"It's alright," she said to him. "You can call me Gwen."

She was friends with his wife, after all. She'd invited them round for dinner tonight.

Dear God, she thought, *dinner*. She'd been shopping, had bought fish.

Who was going to eat that fish now?

She felt her body slump, her head swimming.

Dennis stepped towards her. "Are you alright, Mrs... Gwen?"

She leaned against the wall and pushed herself upright.

"Sorry. I was thinking about the dinner tonight."

His face paled. "I forgot. I'll tell Pam."

She pulled in a shaky breath. "Thanks. Another time, maybe."

He gave her a look of puzzlement, clearly wondering how a woman who'd just lost her husband could think about a dinner party. She frowned at him. Surely he didn't suspect her?

"In fact, it would be nice if Pam could drop by," she said. Her friend had to be better company than the FLO.

He smiled. "Of course. Pam can help you with anything you need."

Gwen knew he was right. Pam would beat any family liaison officer for support and encouragement. Not to mention reporting back to her husband.

But Gwen had nothing to worry about, on that score. It wasn't as if she knew any more than Dennis did about why her husband had died.

"That would be nice," she said.

"Of course. Let's go through into the living room, I can update you on the case." She glanced towards the window. There were journalists outside. One had knocked on the door earlier and she'd finally been glad of the FLO. Now, they were in their cars. Waiting.

Dennis turned to PC Kane. "Two cups of tea, plenty of sugar."

Gwen followed him into the living room, wondering when Dennis Frampton had decided she took sugar in her tea.

CHAPTER NINETEEN

THE ROAD back to Winfrith was a windy one, forcing Dennis to concentrate as he drove. The focus was good for him; he needed to stop thinking about those photos of DCI Mackie lying at the bottom of the cliff.

Gwen had behaved exactly as he'd have expected a new widow to do. She'd alternated between quiet and expressive, numb and upset.

Dennis wondered how Pam would react if it was him. Would her usual brisk efficiency kick in, or would she be devastated? He wasn't sure which of those he preferred.

A thought came to him. He slammed on the brakes, then checked his rear-view mirror. *Christ man, what was that about?* Dennis was a good driver. He'd never done anything like that before, and thank heavens there was nobody behind him this time.

The car had stalled. He started it up again and drove to the next layby.

He parked, his breathing heavy, and turned off the ignition.

He placed his hands on the steering wheel and stared over the fields towards Wool. His head was heavy, his mouth dry. He would need to tell Carpenter about his planned meeting with DCI Mackie. It would help them ascertain a time of death. Mackie not showing up meant that he was probably already dead by then.

Dennis felt a shiver run down his back. Had Mackie been lying there dead all afternoon while Dennis had been dealing with that pathetic burglary in Blandford Forum? Or worse: had Mackie been alive, slowly dying of his injuries?

Dennis squeezed his eyes shut. It didn't bear thinking about.

Be professional, man.

There was an investigation to manage, and even if it was unlikely it would turn into a murder investigation, he had to be prepared.

He gritted his teeth and turned the key in the ignition. He would tell Carpenter, he had to. No matter that he shouldn't have been involving Mackie in his case. This was more important.

He gripped the steering wheel and turned out of the layby, only remembering to check his mirrors as he swerved into the road. He muttered at himself, confused and annoyed.

What was happening to him?

CHAPTER TWENTY

Gail stood at the top of the cliffs, looking out to sea. Behind her, Gavin and Brett were going over the clifftop one last time. The rain had stopped at last and they were desperate to get a proper look, although she knew that last night's storm had probably blown away any evidence.

They'd taken boot prints from all of the attending officers, so they could eliminate those. The line of footprints leading towards the edge was still clear. If those were Mackie's prints, he'd come up here when the ground was wet. And he'd been alone.

She dialled Whittaker: voicemail.

"Doctor, it's Gail Hansford. Can you let me have a photograph of Mackie's shoes when you remove them for the post-mortem, please? It's urgent."

She skirted around the grass, keeping away from those prints, and looked over at the vegetation leading down towards the rocks.

The cliffs here weren't as steep as further along by Old Harry Rocks. There was a slope, shrubs growing out of the clay. It was certainly treacherous. But if you were going to throw yourself over this stretch of coastline, you'd pick the stretch towards the north, surely.

If you wanted to kill yourself here, and chose this particular section of cliff, you could quite easily just end up falling into the shrubs. Which might mean death by exposure, or simply the humiliation of being spotted by the next walker to come along.

DCI Mackie, why did you pick this spot?

The prints indicated that he'd walked to the edge and then thrown himself off. But he would have needed to jump with some force and at quite an angle. The acceleration on the approach would have left tracks in the grass, and divots at the point where he pushed off and hurled himself out over the cliff. There was no sign of any such disturbance. Instead, there were clean footprints leading up to the edge, even and symmetrical. Brett had taken casts of those prints and she would be examining them in detail back at the lab.

She placed large protective plates on the ground to spread her weight and approached the line of prints. She peered into them, examining their edges. They weren't as neat as they looked. Some were ragged around the edges. But it had rained nonstop for eighteen hours. She couldn't expect them to be neat.

Gail backed away, her footsteps careful and her eyes on the prints. They didn't make sense. Hopefully once she'd done a lab analysis, it would become clearer.

CHAPTER TWENTY-ONE

THE MEETING ROOM had been taken from them and Dennis had finally shed his reluctance to use the DCI's office. Mike had brought in the board, the crime scene photos and scribbled notes. It needed to be tidier, but Dennis didn't have the heart to improve it.

He, Johnny, and Mike were in the room. Dennis and Johnny had taken the two chairs opposite the desk, while Mike stood beside the board. Mike was talking over the postmortem report. Nobody had taken the DCI's chair.

Dennis looked up to see the outer door to the office open: Superintendent Carpenter. He went to the door of the DCI's office.

"Can I help you, Sir?"

"A word, please."

Carpenter glanced towards the two DCs. Dennis jerked his head sideways for them to leave the DCI's office and they returned to their desks.

Dennis stood back for Carpenter to enter the room, then closed the door behind the two of them.

"Has something happened, Sir?"

Carpenter shook his head and leaned against the desk.

"I see you've got the board up and running. You're using the office, then?"

"Yes, Sir," Dennis replied. "I hope that's alright."

"Of course it is."

Carpenter peered at the board. Dennis still didn't like using the office of the victim for the investigation into that same man's death.

"You do realise this is probably suicide," Carpenter said.

"We can't be sure until we have more evidence."

Carpenter grunted. "Anyway, there's a DI coming in from Hampshire, DI Jacobi."

"Very good."

Dennis knew of DI Jacobi but had never met him. The man had been on Mackie's team before Mackie had switched to Major Crimes and Jacobi had moved counties.

Dennis hoped that having worked with Mackie, Jacobi would have the correct degree of sensitivity.

"Can I ask when he'll be starting, Sir?"

"Monday, I believe," Carpenter replied. "So in the meantime, I want to sit in on your briefings. You need a senior officer overseeing things."

"I'm sure that won't be necessary, Sir."

Carpenter shook his head. "I shall be sitting in. Call the DCs back in, would you?"

Dennis stiffened. He walked to the door, his movements slow. He didn't want Carpenter to witness his unease at the senior officer's presence. But he was too agitated to hide his reaction.

"Johnny, Mike," he said, "can you come into the office please?"

CHAPTER TWENTY-ONE

Johnny looked through the glass towards Carpenter, who had taken the DCI's old chair.

"Everything alright?" he asked.

"Everything's fine, Johnny," Dennis replied. "Let's just continue with the briefing."

CHAPTER TWENTY-TWO

Carpenter smiled at Dennis, waiting for him to speak. As the two DCs took their seats, Gail entered the outer office. She strode to the office and opened the door.

"You got a moment?" she asked.

Dennis nodded towards Carpenter and Gail shrugged. She wasn't bothered by the super.

"DS Frampton was about to go over the evidence," Carpenter said. "Join us."

Gail raised her eyebrows at Dennis, who said nothing.

Carpenter was still in the DCI's old chair. Gail shuffled past Dennis and took a spot in the corner towards the back.

"Very well," Dennis began. "Let's recap on what we have. Before we start, I need to let you know that we're going to have a new senior investigating officer, DI Jacobi, from Hampshire. He worked with DCI Mackie in the past, which makes him well qualified to manage this investigation."

Carpenter nodded and crossed his ankle over his knee.

Johnny and Mike shook their heads. Gail nodded. "He's good," she said. "If anybody's going to get a result..."

CHAPTER TWENTY-TWO

"That might not be too difficult," Carpenter said. Dennis looked at him but the super had nothing more to add.

"Mike," Dennis said. "What do we have from the PM?"

"No surprise on the cause of death." Mike shuffled in his chair. "He broke his neck when he hit the rocks."

Dennis closed his eyes momentarily.

"He was alive until he hit the ground?" he asked as he opened them again.

Mike looked at his hands, still in his lap. "Yes."

"What about toxicology?"

"Nothing, Sarge. He was clean."

So Mackie had been of sound mind when he'd fallen to his death. Dennis tried not to think about how that would have felt.

"Any signs of a struggle?" Johnny asked. "Defensive wounds?"

"Nothing." Mike rubbed under his nose. "Just the injuries from the fall."

The room fell silent. After a moment, Gail spoke.

"I've just come from the cliffs. It doesn't feel right to me."

"Go on," Dennis said.

Gail pulled the strap of her shoulder bag over her head and placed it on the floor. She fished inside it and brought out an envelope. Inside were two photographs which she pinned to the board. Both of them showed the edge of the cliff, the view from the top.

"These shrubs here," she said. "They're directly in the line between the shoe prints and the spot where Mackie was found."

She looked at Carpenter and then back at Dennis.

"I'm concerned about the force with which a person would have to throw themselves off the cliff in order to clear them. There's damage to the shrubs, but even so, the very fact that he didn't get caught on them makes me wonder."

"Makes you wonder what?" Carpenter said.

Dennis turned towards him. Johnny and Mike straightened in their seats.

"Makes me wonder if he was pushed," Gail replied.

"But the prints," Johnny said. "They only lead in one direction."

Carpenter uncrossed his ankle. "Are you sure you aren't clutching at straws here? I know we're all very sad at what's happened, but—"

"I have a theory," Gail said.

Carpenter raised an eyebrow. "Enlighten us."

Gail stepped towards the board. She pointed at the footprints in the photograph.

"These prints are perfect. Too perfect."

"I don't see how evidence can be *too* good," Carpenter said.

"I didn't say good. I said perfect."

Carpenter stood up. "If that's a—"

"And the shrubs." Gail put a finger on the photo of the clifftop. "If I was going to throw myself off, I would choose that spot there, not this one."

"DCI Mackie may not have been thinking straight," Carpenter said.

"And it was blowing a gale," Mike added.

Gail frowned at Mike. "Those prints seem abnormal to me."

"In what way abnormal?" Dennis asked.

"I'm going to try to recreate the prints from the cast. But I'm not convinced they weren't trodden in more than once."

CHAPTER TWENTY-TWO

"More than once?" Carpenter asked. "What do you mean?"

Dennis looked at the photo. There was just one set of footprints leading towards the cliff edge. It was clear, but then he thought of what Gwen had said to him.

"You think he retraced his steps?" Dennis asked. "That he *didn't* throw himself off the cliff?"

Gail shook her head.

"I don't think they're Mackie's footprints at all. I think somebody else made those prints and then retraced their steps."

Carpenter snorted. "They'd have to be bloody twinkletoes."

Gail shook her head. "I'm going to analyse the cast, try to recreate those prints."

"Have you matched them against DCI Mackie's shoes?" Dennis asked.

She looked at Mike. "Not yet."

"His boots are in the evidence store," said Mike. "I got them from Pathology, there's photos on HOLMES."

Dennis felt a shiver run through him.

"Do we have a time of death?" he asked.

"Lunchtime to mid-afternoon," said Mike.

Dennis put out a hand and brushed the wall. Johnny looked at him and mouthed something. Dennis gave him a nod of reassurance.

Carpenter stood up. "I have to go," he said. "DI Jacobi will be here in two days and he'll wrap things up. It's looking increasingly like DCI Mackie took his own life."

"Very well, Sir," Dennis said.

Carpenter looked between each of the members of the team.

"You carry on as you are," he told them. "I shall be speaking to the coroner in the morning after he's examined the pathology report. I'll let DI Jacobi know what his conclusion is."

CHAPTER TWENTY-THREE

As Dennis slid back into his own chair in the outside office. Gail hesitated by his desk, on her way out.

"Everything alright, Gail?"

She stared towards the door, her lips pursed. After a moment, she shook her head. "Yes. I forgot to say. Gavin's at the house, looking through Mackie's things."

"Poor Mrs Mackie."

"Yes." She shook her head. "I'll let you know if I find anything more about those prints."

"Thank you." Dennis turned on his computer as she left the room.

His phone rang.

"DS Frampton."

"Sarge, it's PC Kane." The family liaison officer.

"Constable," Dennis said. "Everything alright?"

"The CSIs have found something."

"In the house?"

"No, Sarge. In the DCI's car."

Dennis looked up to see the office door open. Gail stood in it, her phone to her ear. She gave him a nod.

"What is it they've found?" Dennis asked.

"A letter, Sarge."

"What kind of letter?"

Dennis watched as Gail put her phone in her pocket. She took a step forward, her gaze still on Dennis.

"What kind of letter?" he repeated into the phone.

"Not a letter, really, Sarge," said the PC. "A note. It's a suicide note."

CHAPTER TWENTY-FOUR

Mike looked up at the sarge's words.

"A suicide note, Sarge?"

DS Frampton nodded. "You two, stay here. Hold the fort while I'm gone."

"I want to get over there," said Gail. "See where it was found. Context is everything."

The sarge looked agitated. "I'm going to the house. I don't want his wife hearing this from the wrong person."

Mike looked at Johnny, whose eyes were on the sarge.

"Anything I can help with?" Johnny asked.

Mike frowned. Johnny would be brought into the heart of the investigation, as always. He'd be left here to run through HOLMES and collate evidence.

As always.

"No," said the sarge. "I already said for you and Mike to stay here."

Johnny shrank back in his chair. Mike watched him, surprised.

"You don't need to come," Gail said. "This is CSI work."

The sarge looked at her. "If DCI Mackie was suicidal, I want to know about it."

Gail shrugged and hurried out, the sarge trailing behind.

Five minutes later, the door opened. Johnny stood up. He was expecting the sarge to have come back for him.

It wasn't the sarge. Instead, a short man with curly red hair hurried in.

Johnny sank to his seat.

"Can I help you?" Mike asked.

The man looked around the office, his movements stiff. His gaze settled on Mike. "Are you DS Frampton?"

Mike exchanged glances with Johnny and stifled a laugh.

"No chance." He stood up. "DC Legg. Can I ask who you are?"

Mike looked at Johnny again. Johnny shrugged. The man frowned and breathed out through his nostrils.

"I'm DI Jacobi. Do you work for DS Frampton?"

Mike straightened. "I do, Sir."

He put out a hand which the DI took, his handshake firm.

"Like I said, I'm DC Legg, and this is DC Chiles. DS Frampton got a call about new evidence, he's gone out."

The DI grunted and pointed in the direction of the inner office. "Is that my office?"

"I'm sorry, Sir. Are you the replacement for DCI Mackie?"

The man looked at him. "I'm from Hampshire Police, I've been brought in temporarily to work on your suspicious death case."

"Oh," Mike said. "Yes."

The DI looked him up and down. "Well done, Constable. Sharp, I can tell."

CHAPTER TWENTY-FOUR

Mike tensed. "I'm sorry, Sir. It was just a little confusing when you came in looking for the DS."

"I'm sure it was. So where will I find him?"

Mike exchanged another glance with Johnny.

"He got a call about a suicide note," Johnny said. "Written by DCI Mackie."

Jacobi's shoulders dropped. "A suicide note. So you don't need me then."

Mike frowned at Johnny. *Why are you leaving all this to me?*

"I wouldn't jump to conclusions just yet, Sir," Mike said.

Jacobi peeled off his coat. "Where do I put this?"

Mike indicated the hooks beside the door and the DI turned and hung up his coat. The man was short and had to stretch. Mike looked at Johnny, who was mouthing something at him. Mike shrugged.

He turned back as Jacobi approached.

"Right," the DI said. "I'll be in my office. I'll give DS Frampton a call."

CHAPTER TWENTY-FIVE

Dennis sat in an armchair in the Mackies' sitting room, his feet shuffling on the carpet beneath him. He could hear Gwen Mackie in the kitchen next door, running water. She'd offered him a cup of tea and he'd accepted. It gave both of them a chance to get used to the fact that he was here.

His phone buzzed: Gail.

I'm sending you a photo of the note.

Good. That would give him time to look at it before Gwen came back in.

He watched his phone, occasionally glancing up at the door. He heard the kettle click off and the sound of cupboard doors opening and closing.

Hurry up.

His phone buzzed again. He opened the first photo, his palms sweating. There were two of them: one of the front, one of the back. He scanned them, reading the text.

The handwriting was in blue fountain pen, large and loopy. He recognised it.

CHAPTER TWENTY-FIVE

Dennis felt a shiver travel over his skin. So his old boss had killed himself after all.

He'd been so desperate that he'd written a note and thrown himself off a cliff.

The door opened and Gwen entered, holding a tray with two mugs and a plate of biscuits. The FLO trailed behind her, shrugging an apology to Dennis.

"Have you got news?" Gwen asked as she placed the tray down.

"Mrs Mackie," he began.

"Gwen."

"Gwen. There's been a development."

"Oh?"

"We found your husband's car."

"Where?"

"A car park, in Swanage." Not the one they'd arranged to meet in. Not the one near the DCI's usual pub.

"Oh," she repeated. "Near where they… where they found him?"

He shook his head. There were two car parks closer to the spot where they'd found Mackie's body. Instead, his car had been left in the car park at Durlston Head, on the opposite side of the town.

"That isn't all though, Mrs… Gwen."

"Oh." She put her hand on the side table next to her, scraping the wood with her fingernails.

He swallowed. "I'm sorry to tell you this. But inside the car, we found a note left by your husband."

Her hand brushed against a mug, almost toppling it. Dennis reached out but the mug righted itself before he got to it.

"A note?" Her voice was faint.

He gave her a stiff smile. "Your husband left a note saying he was planning to kill himself."

CHAPTER TWENTY-SIX

As Dennis walked away from the Mackie house, he realised his heart was pounding.

Gwen had been distraught, breaking down in tears when he told her the news. He realised that both of them had been assuming DCI Mackie's death had been an accident. A suspicion had nagged at him that there might be something more sinister at the heart of it, but this was Swanage, and nobody wanted DCI Mackie dead.

The man had retired, and was happy about it. His health was good, his marriage solid. Dennis had hoped that he'd taken a fall, maybe lost his footing during a clifftop walk.

But who would go for a walk in yesterday's weather? And those footprints...

He jumped at the sound of a car door closing behind him. A young woman with blonde hair hurried away from it and towards him. He ignored her.

"Detective Sergeant Frampton?"

He turned, despite himself. How did she know his name?

"Who are you?"

She held up a pass on the end of a lanyard. "Sadie Dawes, BBC News. Did DCI Mackie commit suicide, or are you launching a murder investigation?"

He looked towards the house. "Leave his poor widow alone, will you? She doesn't need you hanging around."

The journalist looked at him. "If you could tell me what direction the investigation is going in, then I'll be out of your hair."

He narrowed his eyes, not believing a word of it. "There will be an official statement when we're in a position to release more information. Now, if you don't mind…"

Dennis hurried to his car and slammed the door. His breathing was heavy. The woman was still out there.

Vultures.

He started the ignition. He didn't like leaving Gwen Mackie to them, but she had PC Kane, and he needed to get away from here.

After driving for five minutes, he found a layby and pulled over. Staring out of the windscreen, he let his mind wander.

He couldn't fathom it. Mackie, who'd been so disparaging towards people who killed themselves and left the emergency services to pick up the pieces. He'd done the very same thing himself.

The note was clear. *I've been suffering depression for some months. I can't imagine my future. I don't want to be here anymore. I'm so sorry.*

Dennis slumped forward and placed his hands on the steering wheel, his knuckles pale. He sat and stared out of the front window, blinking from time to time.

His phone was buzzing. It had been buzzing while he was talking to the journalist.

CHAPTER TWENTY-SIX

He swallowed and held it up. Two missed calls. One from Mike, the other from Pam. He dialled voicemail. Pam's message was first.

"Hello, love, just ringing to check what time you'll be home. I'm making a stew, lamb, your favourite. Call me when you're on your way home, yes? I've been missing you."

There was an edge to her voice: she'd been thinking about Gwen Mackie. His chest felt heavy.

The voicemail clicked onto the next message.

"Sarge, it's Mike. The new SIO has turned up, DI Jacobi. Johnny and I didn't know he'd be here yet, we were... well, I don't think we created the best first impression. He's trying to get hold of you, just wanted to let you know."

Dennis hung up. He took a few breaths, then checked his texts. Sure enough, there was one from DI Jacobi.

He dialled the number, straightening his back as he did so.

"Jacobi," came the response.

"Sir, this is DS Frampton. I'm sorry I wasn't in the office when you arrived this afternoon."

"That's alright, Sergeant. I've heard you were out following up a lead."

"Are you taking over as SIO?" Dennis asked him.

"That depends."

"Oh. On?"

"On this suicide note. Your CSM has sent me a copy. Looks like you don't need me after all."

Dennis frowned. The suicide note looked conclusive, he had to admit it.

His own assumptions about Mackie's motives were nothing compared to evidence. A man desperate enough to jump off the cliffs wouldn't be thinking about his old colleagues.

Dennis closed his eyes.

"Do you need me to come into the office, Sir? I imagine we need to—"

"Don't bother," the DI replied. "It's getting on, you go home. We'll reconvene in the morning. I imagine I'll be out of your hair by lunchtime tomorrow."

The DI hung up. Dennis dropped his phone into his lap and stared at it.

Home, he thought. Was he going to tell Pam what they'd found?

No, not yet. Not until he knew more.

CHAPTER TWENTY-SEVEN

"Good morning, everybody," said DI Jacobi. "We won't bother with introductions, seeing as I'll be gone by the end of today."

Dennis realised that the two DCs were looking at him. He gave them each a reassuring nod, then looked back at the DI.

Jacobi sat in DCI Mackie's chair, leaning back, his fingers entwined behind his head. Dennis didn't like the way he was making himself so comfortable. But as the man had said, he would be gone by the end of the day.

Jacobi stood up, almost sending the chair flying. He strode to the board. Dennis, Johnny and Mike turned, watching him. He stopped at the board and took a photo from it.

"Mackie's suicide note," he said. "The man told us what happened, he left us a message."

Dennis cleared his throat. "Strictly speaking, Sir, he left his wife a message."

"Has she seen it?"

"Not yet. We're waiting until it's been verified."

Jacobi frowned at Dennis. "It's a suicide note and there's no reason to doubt it. The coroner has a copy of it."

"What about the pathologist, Sir?" asked Mike.

Jacobi turned to him. "The pathologist's findings are consistent with suicide."

Dennis felt his vision blur over. Jacobi was right. Broken neck, no defensive wounds.

"What about the boot prints?" asked Mike. "Gail was—"

Dennis shook his head at Mike. *Not now*.

"Very well then," said Jacobi, as if Mike hadn't said a word. "The coroner will be making his report tomorrow. To be honest, I don't know why Carpenter hauled me over here."

Dennis swallowed. He looked away from the DI, staring towards the now empty chair. He had a recurring memory of a conversation he'd had with Mackie a month before the DCI had retired. They'd been discussing Mackie's plans, the things he'd intended to do with Gwen after retiring. Mackie had been going on about dance floors. He'd urged Dennis to take early retirement so he could do the same with Pam. Not ballroom dancing, of course. Hill walking was more their thing. But Dennis had three and a half years left, and he wanted to get his full pension.

He swallowed, his body stiff. Despite all that, Mackie had killed himself. A suicide note and no defensive wounds. Boot prints leading to the cliff edge, none coming back.

He still found it difficult to believe the DCI would have left a mess for his colleagues to clear up.

But if he was that desperate? Desperate enough to lie to everybody, to book a cruise as cover for how he was really feeling?

CHAPTER TWENTY-SEVEN

If DCI Mackie had confided in him, would he have been able to help?

He doubted it. He was just a work colleague.

"DS Frampton."

Dennis looked up to see Jacobi standing in front of him, head cocked.

"You alright, Sergeant?"

Dennis sat up straight. "I'm fine, Sir. Just coming to terms with the reality of this case."

Jacobi raised his eyebrows. "A suicide is far better than a suspicious death, surely?"

"Perhaps," replied Dennis.

CHAPTER TWENTY-EIGHT

"Where is he?" Gail asked as she stormed into the office.

Dennis looked up. "Who?"

"Your new DI, the guy from Hampshire."

Dennis looked towards the office, but he knew the answer.

"He's in with the super," he said. "Wrapping up the case."

"Wrapping up the case?" Gail asked. "Yesterday you said there was no way DCI Mackie would kill himself, today you're accepting a suicide?"

"Your people found the note," Dennis replied.

"The sarge is right, Gail," Johnny added. "You can't argue with a suicide note."

"Have you got a copy?" Gail snapped.

"There's a photo on the board," Dennis said.

She pushed open the door to Mackie's office and strode towards the board. Dennis followed her, his breathing shallow.

CHAPTER TWENTY-EIGHT

"Gail," he said. "What are you—?"

She turned to him.

"This isn't Tim Mackie's office anymore, Dennis," she said. "You have to get used to the fact that we can come in here without permission."

He swallowed.

"The copy's on the board, as I told you."

"I can see it."

She tore the photo off the board and peered at it.

"I want to get a graphologist on this," she said. "Check that it's his writing."

"You think it's a fake?"

"It could be."

"Really?"

She stared at him. "Do you think Tim Mackie was the sort of man who would have killed himself?"

Dennis's throat was tight. "No, but—"

"But, nothing." She waved the photo in his face. "I'll tell you when I get a result."

"You won't get it in time," he told her. "The coroner's reporting later today."

"Today? What the fu—"

"Gail," Dennis warned.

"Come on then," she told him. "Find your lousy swear jar, I'll put a quid in it, and then I can say whatever the hell I like."

Dennis realised that Johnny was standing behind him, the swear jar in his hand. Gail delved in her pocket, brought out a pound coin, and shoved it inside.

"There," she said, staring into Dennis's face. Then she crumpled.

"I'm sorry, Dennis. I've just..." She sighed. "I'll get the graphologist to analyse this, coroner or no coroner. I'm convinced it won't be DCI Mackie's writing."

CHAPTER TWENTY-NINE

Gwen heaved herself up from the chair at the sound of the doorbell.

"It's alright, Mrs Mackie," came the voice of the family liaison officer. "I've got it."

Gwen sighed and sat back down. She was trying to do some knitting, but couldn't concentrate. She'd already dropped three stitches and was going to have to redo this entire row.

She plunged it into her lap, wondering who was at the door. After a moment, she heard voices in the hallway. A man talking to the family liaison officer.

She recognised that voice. Like cut glass.

She bundled the knitting up and placed it on the coffee table. She stood up, smoothing her hands on her trousers and turned towards the door of the living room. The FLO opened it, smiling at her.

"Superintendent Carpenter for you, Mrs Mackie."

She swallowed and forced a smile. Her lips had been chewed so much they were swollen, and she knew that her face was blotchy. She hadn't put on makeup this morning or yesterday.

"Superintendent," she said.

He smiled at her. "Call me Anthony," he said, walking into the room with an air of confidence. "Mind if I sit down?"

She nodded and watched him take the space next to where she'd been sitting on the sofa. She took a step back and lowered herself into the armchair, glancing at her knitting as she did so. As badly as it was going, she'd still rather do that than talk to Carpenter.

"What can I help you with?" she asked him.

He gave her another one of those smiles, the sort that made her feel queasy.

"It's more what I can help you with," he replied, his voice smooth. "I have some news."

"Go on," she said.

"The coroner has finished his deliberations and released his report."

Carpenter dipped his head, his lips tight. She imagined the impression was calculated to convey sympathy, but instead it just looked odd.

"I'm afraid your husband took his own life," he continued. "The coroner's verdict will be suicide."

She nodded. "The note."

He pursed his lips, his hands shifting in his lap.

"The crime scene manager wants to have it analysed by graphologists," he said. "To be sure that it is your husband's writing." He licked his lips. "But can I ask...?"

"You want me to look at it?" she said. "You want me to tell you if it's his writing?"

He nodded, glancing at the family liaison officer.

CHAPTER TWENTY-NINE

"Constable, fetch my briefcase from the hallway, will you?"

The PC nodded and left the room.

"Are you sure you're up to this?" he asked Gwen.

She stared back at him. She didn't want this man to know how hard she was finding this. Tim had told her how he felt about people who committed suicide. The selfishness of it, leaving other people to clear up. Sometimes figuratively, sometimes literally.

She couldn't believe that Tim had brought himself to do that. He'd booked a cruise, for God's sake.

"Yes," she said, her voice tight. "Show me the letter, please."

She felt her voice catch on the last word. The FLO was behind her. She held the letter out and the superintendent snatched it. He laid it on the coffee table, next to Gwen's knitting.

She drew in a breath. She looked up at the ceiling, then down at the coffee table. All it took was a glance at the words.

"Yes," she said. "That's Tim's writing."

CHAPTER THIRTY

Dennis stood at the back of the church, his eyes on Gwen Mackie. She stood stiffly at the front, her gaze straight ahead, her expression stiff. She was trying not to cry, he could tell.

He knew that feeling. Pam had asked him if he wanted her to accompany him, but he knew that if she was here, clutching his hand, he would break down.

A woman he didn't recognise stood next to Gwen, her arm on the woman's back. She was slightly taller than Mrs Mackie, but had the same firm set to her jaw. A sister, perhaps. She rubbed Gwen's shoulder and Gwen shook, just slightly.

They all stood at the sound of movement behind them, the pallbearers entering with the coffin. Dennis had volunteered, but Carpenter had overruled him. He wanted senior officers alongside Mackie's brother and adult son. Dennis watched as the six men carried the coffin to the front of the church.

There was a sob from the front: Gwen.

Poor woman. What must it be like to know your husband

CHAPTER THIRTY

had been that desperate? To learn, too late, that he was so unhappy he would lie to you? Mackie had fabricated a whole future that he didn't intend to share with her, and then ripped it away from her with just a handwritten note.

A woman walked in, a few steps behind the pallbearers, trying not to draw attention to herself. Dennis rolled his eyes: trust Gail to be late.

She slipped into the back row next to him.

"I hope nobody noticed me," she muttered.

He grunted. "I was wondering if you'd come."

"Of *course* I came. I wanted to pay my respects."

He nodded, his lips tight. *Hold it together*, he told himself. He would be fine.

"I got the graphologist's report back," Gail whispered.

He twitched, irritated. Now wasn't the time.

"It was his writing," she said. "The characteristics were all there."

"His wife already told Carpenter it was his writing," he hissed. "I don't see why you needed to do that."

"I wanted a second opinion," she told him. "I'm still not convinced."

He leaned towards her.

"Drop it, Gail," he said. "It doesn't help anybody for you to drag this out. Mackie killed himself, he lied to us all. None of us knew what state he was in, and then he killed himself."

She looked back at him and shook her head. "I still don't believe it."

"You have to," he told her. "It's easier for all of us if you do."

Somebody in the row ahead cleared his throat and looked around, his face hard.

"Shush," Dennis said.

"You're the one talking," Gail whispered back at him.

He said nothing.

He didn't want her standing next to him, he didn't want to talk to her.

He just wanted all this to be over.

CHAPTER THIRTY-ONE

Dennis had his key up, about to insert it into the lock, when Pam opened the door. He dropped his hand to his side and gazed at her. She cocked her head and gave him a sympathetic smile.

"How was it, love?"

"Tough," he said, closing his eyes.

She put a hand on his shoulder.

"Come in, I'll make you a nice cup of tea. I've baked some scones, your favourite."

He smiled at her.

"You're too good to me."

She raised an eyebrow.

"I know," she said. "That's because I don't want to lose you."

He closed the front door behind him and reached out to pull her into an embrace.

"You're never going to lose me, Pam. You don't have to worry."

She didn't meet his eye. "That's what Gwen thought."

"I'm not Tim Mackie," he told her. "I'm not depressed. I'm not suicidal."

She pushed him away.

"That's what everybody thought about him. Gwen's distraught, she can't believe that he didn't confide in her."

Dennis grabbed her hand. "He didn't confide in any of us."

"When was the last time you saw him?" she asked.

"Ten days ago," he said. "I met him for a pint, and then we spoke just over a week ago. We were supposed to be meeting to talk about a case, but he didn't turn up."

"Was that the day he—?"

"I don't want to talk about it."

Pam brought his hand up to her cheek.

"You have to talk about it, love," she said. "If you don't, you'll end up like him."

He pulled his hand down. "I won't," he told her. "That's ridiculous. I'm fine. Now where's that cup of tea?"

CHAPTER THIRTY-TWO

It was a Sunday lunchtime six weeks after Mackie's death when Dennis got the call. He'd just arrived home with Pam and was about to carve the roast lamb that had been cooking while they'd been at church.

"I'm sorry, love," he told her. "There's been an emergency in Corfe Castle."

"What kind of emergency?" she asked. "On a Sunday lunchtime?"

"Someone's reported a body," he said.

She looked at him. She was wearing a blue dress, the one that brought out the colour of her eyes. It made her look slimmer. Younger, too.

He stroked her face.

"I won't be long. I'm sure it's nothing, probably just a drunk or something."

"But if they said it's a body," she replied. "A murder maybe?"

He laughed. "Don't be ridiculous, it's Corfe Castle."

She gave him a dry smile.

"You get on with it then, I'll keep your lunch warm."

He kissed her and hurried out of the house. Twenty minutes later he was parking on the verge of the Lulworth road, below Corfe Castle. A squad car and ambulance had already arrived.

He slammed his car door closed, wondering if he should change into his walking boots.

But he could hear voices beyond the hedge, and it hadn't rained for the last couple of days.

He straightened his jacket and made for the sound of the voices. Beyond the hedge, a paramedic was approaching, guiding a young blonde woman. The woman was moaning, leaning on the paramedic.

He stood back for the paramedic to pass with the woman, pushed through a gap in the hedge, lifting his elbows to protect his face. Ahead of him, a girl sat on the ground next to the two PCs Dennis recognised from the cliffs above where they'd found Mackie. Beyond them were two tents.

Dennis frowned. Forensic tents, when the CSIs hadn't arrived yet?

He approached the tents. A woman stood in the doorway of one, her back to him. Dennis realised these weren't forensic tents.

One of the PCs, the man, approached him. "Sarge."

"What's happened? The ambulance?"

"Ambulance has got a witness in it, Sarge. She found a body."

Dennis's gaze followed the PC's outstretched arm towards the closest tent. The tall blonde woman was approaching them, her stride hurried. He steeled himself.

"Forensics got that up already?" he asked. "I'm impressed."

CHAPTER THIRTY-TWO

"It's an archaeological dig, Sarge," the PC said. "The King Stephen investigation at the Rings."

Dennis knew nothing about King Stephen or an investigation. But he did know that the blonde woman had stopped in front of him and folded her arms, looking impatient.

"Er, excuse me?" she said.

He pulled in a breath. "Madam. We'll be right with you, take a statement." The female PC was behind her; he nodded at her. "See to it, will you?"

The female PC looked at the woman then back at him.

What are you waiting for?

"What's your name, Sergeant?" the woman asked. She wore a pair of walking trousers and a fleece that didn't fit.

"Frampton. You don't need me, PC Abbott can take your statement." He turned away, making for the tent. He ignored the muttering behind him.

As he neared the tent, he felt movement behind him.

"Are you CID? It's a Sunday, maybe you're off duty."

He turned to see the woman right behind him, surveying him like he was a pound of ham.

"You look like CID," she said.

Dennis bristled. "Yes, Madam. I'm CID."

"In that case, let me introduce myself." She held out a pale hand. "DCI Lesley Clarke. I start in the Major Crimes Investigation Team tomorrow morning. You could say I jumped in early."

What?

He straightened. "Ma'am."

The female PC, standing next to him now, stifled a smirk. Dennis looked back at the woman. DCI Clarke. His new boss.

Why hadn't anyone warned him?

I hope you enjoyed reading *The Ballard Down Murder*. The first book in the Dorset Crime series is *The Corfe Castle Murders*, which you can buy from book retailers or via my website.

Happy reading! Rachel McLean

READ THE DORSET CRIME SERIES

The Corfe Castle Murders
The Clifftop Murders
The Island Murders
The Monument Murders
The Millionaire Murders
The Fossil Beach Murders
The Blue Pool Murders
The Lighthouse Murders
The Ghost Village Murders
The Poole Harbour Murders
The Chesil Beach Murders

Buy from book retailers or via the Rachel McLean website.

ALSO BY RACHEL MCLEAN

The DI Zoe Finch Series – buy from book retailers or via the Rachel McLean website.

Deadly Wishes

Deadly Choices

Deadly Desires

Deadly Terror

Deadly Reprisal

Deadly Fallout

Deadly Christmas

Deadly Origins, the FREE Zoe Finch prequel

The McBride & Tanner Series – Buy from book retailers or via the Rachel McLean website.

Blood and Money

Death and Poetry

Power and Treachery

Secrets and History

The Cumbria Crime Series by Rachel McLean and Joel Hames – Buy from book retailers or via the Rachel McLean website.

The Harbour

The Mine

The Cairn

The Barn

The Lake

The Wood

The Port

...and more to come

Read the London Cosy Mystery Series by Rachel McLean and Millie Ravensworth – Buy from book retailers or via the Rachel McLean website.

Death at Westminster

Death in the West End

Death at Tower Bridge

Death on the Thames

Death at St Paul's Cathedral

Death at Abbey Road

The Lyme Regis Women's Swimming Club series by Rachel McLean and Millie Ravensworth – buy from book retailers or via the Rachel McLean website.

The Lyme Regis Women's Swimming Club

A Brush with Death

...and more to come

Printed and bound by CPI Group (UK) Ltd, Croydon, CR0 4YY

17/04/2026

02092053-0002